The Other Princess

Cowboy Fairytales: The Next Generation

Lacy Williams

Prologue

"You're too nice."

Maggie Hale groaned and dropped her head into her hands. "Not this again."

She was seated across the nook table from her cousin Scarlett in the original Triple H ranch house, where Scarlett and her husband Miles lived. The remnants of breakfast—biscuit crumbs, the empty gravy bowl, a few scrambled egg curds, and a plate with a lone piece of bacon—were spread out between them.

Maggie needed more coffee if her cousin was going to keep spouting nonsense.

Scarlett pointed her fork. "Everyone knows the ranch house is the best place to live, but you and Uncle Gideon built that bungalow down by the stock pond. *Nice.*"

"You were here first." Maggie stood and went to the coffeepot. Thankfully, Scarlett made industrial-strength French Roast. Outside the window, dawn was lighting the sky with streaks of silver.

Maggie liked the bungalow. It was small. Cozy.

"Miles and I were here first," Scarlett said, "but you're royalty. You could've kicked us out."

As if Maggie needed to be reminded that she couldn't be just plain old Maggie. She was Princess Margaret, fifth in line for the throne of Glorvaird.

She would never think to kick Scarlett and Miles out of their home. An exclamation stating just that was on the tip of Maggie's tongue, but if she uttered it, she'd just prove her cousin was right. Scarlett and Miles and their toddler daughter Richelle lived in the ranch house with Scarlett's mom, Maggie's Aunt Carrie, and her stepdad Trey. It was a multi-generational household that worked for them.

Scarlett swiped the last piece of bacon as Maggie approached the table warily. She pointed it at Maggie. "Too nice." And crunched into the crispy goodness.

"Hey!" Maggie's protest was halfhearted. She knew better than to try and keep food from a pregnant woman. Scarlett's baby bump—this was her second child—was barely noticeable, and they hadn't announced anything yet, but Maggie had been around for Scarlett's first pregnancy and knew the signs.

Frequent irritability, food cravings, know-it-all-ness. That one was pure Scarlett, though, pregnant or not.

"I am nice," Maggie admitted, because Scarlett was partly right. She was nice, but she wasn't *too* nice. "But that has nothing to do with getting the charity board to fund this riding program."

The therapeutic riding program was Maggie's heart-project. Getting it off the ground was the one thing she wanted to accomplish before she turned thirty in five years.

Horses had been her refuge when she'd needed one the most. And there were so many kids out there dealing with anxiety, abandonment, being bullied.

Her program could help.

She just needed the other board members to buy in.

"You need to throw your weight around," Scarlett said. "Wear your tiara to the next board meeting and remind those old geezers who you are. *You* started the foundation."

Technically, Maggie's dad had started it when she'd been nineteen. He'd told her he wanted her to run it. And since he rarely asked her for anything, she'd agreed.

It had been her first time into Dallas since—

In the other room, the back door opened and closed. Probably one of the hands stomping into the mudroom to report to Scarlett, who acted as foreman for the cattle operation.

But it wasn't a cowboy who appeared.

It was Maggie's mirror-image. Her twin, who hadn't visited the Triple H Ranch in at least five years.

"Tirith. What are you doing here?"

Chapter One

This was never going to work.

Maggie wobbled across the carpeted expanse of her sister's living room, tilting and twisting on heels that felt like stilts. The palace walls were thick stone and would muffle any sounds she made.

She was no rodeo clown, but she'd probably get some laughs if she tried to wear these heels and pitched hiney over teakettle in front of the photographers who followed her family around any time they stepped foot out of the royal palace.

Muttering words that were certainly not suitable for her station, Maggie peeled off one torture device and then the other—otherwise known as Louboutins.

She retraced her steps back to her sister's bedroom. Before yesterday, she'd never been in this suite. It'd been well over a decade since she'd stepped foot on Glorvaird soil. Even the suite they'd shared as children would've felt foreign.

This morning, Tirith's personal assistant Elizabeth had laid out the plum-colored pantsuit, white silk blouse, and offending shoes while Maggie had been showering.

The clothes whispered along her skin, the softness almost as foreign as having someone choose her outfit, down to the diamond cuff bracelet that felt like a shackle around her wrist.

And that was a drop in the bucket of discomfort after Maggie had been subjected to nearly an hour in a chair getting her hair, makeup and manicure done before she'd been allowed to dress.

The stylist had been aghast at the state of her hair. She hadn't had the heart to tell him that the highlights he was griping about were natural from being out in the sun all day. At least the manicurist had been silent in her judgment of Maggie's farm-girl hands.

Had they already figured it out? Would they go to the press?

Maybe she wouldn't even last the first morning of this charade.

She stomped back to the bedroom, shoes in hand. The crowd of *helpers*—more like handlers—had made themselves scarce after she'd been adequately groomed, and she now had the suite to herself.

She'd spent close to an hour last night practicing in the mirror, trying to get Tirith down. They might be twins, but Tirith was practically a stranger to her. How she stood, how she walked... if Maggie messed it up, this crazy plan would be over. She'd had deportment lessons from an instructor her mother had sent to the Triple H when Maggie was thirteen. That was twelve years ago, and she'd never had an occasion to use what she'd begrudgingly learned. She'd skipped senior prom in favor of going camping with her dad.

Now she went straight to the walk-in closet—bigger than her room back at home—and stepped inside. Flats. She just needed a pair of flats that matched this suit.

She blinked at the array of clothes in every color, each one with a designer label. Nothing like what filled her closet back home.

Even blinking felt wrong. Her eyelashes were Tirith's, not hers. Curled with a wicked-looking silver tool, painted with mascara and lined with a pencil.

She should have probably been thankful the stylist hadn't given her false eyelashes.

Being Tirith was the whole point.

She sighed as she left the heels right in the middle of the closet floor and went to the set of shelves built into the very back of the space.

There. The ballet flats were plain black, and Maggie knew she could make it through the day without falling on her face if she wore them. She quickly slipped them on.

"Just be Tirith," she said under her breath as she went back through the bedroom and into the living area.

It was easier said than done. Her sister didn't even have a television, only bookshelves that lined one entire wall.

Maggie enjoyed curling up with a good book as much as anybody, but come on. Sometimes a girl needed a few hours of college football to unwind. There was something therapeutic about booing the referee when he made a terrible call. Dad kept several of last year's best games on the DVR for when they needed a fix during the off season.

The sleek orange cat tiptoed out of Tirith's bedroom door and into the bathroom. The second sighting Maggie had had of it. It must've slept under the bed. Or in the closet. Probably waiting to pounce.

Of course Tirith had a cat.

Maggie was a dog person.

She gritted her teeth.

She'd make do. It was only for two weeks.

She grimaced, then caught a glimpse of her face in the wall-mounted mirror across the room.

When was the last time Tirith had asked her for anything?

Never.

Not since they'd been taken—

Maggie couldn't let herself go there. Not when she was this close. There was a reason she'd stayed in Texas for so long.

But her twin needed her. And Tirith never needed anything. She was strong. So much stronger than Maggie.

The fact that Tirith had asked for help now meant she needed it desperately. How could Maggie say no?

She left the suite, forcing herself to walk with the same forbidding posture Tirith used. She wanted to run her fingers along the stone walls, remember their texture. Something else she'd forgotten in her long absence. She wanted to wander over to what had been the nursery when she and Tirith had been infants. Surely the cribs they'd slept in were gone by now. Or maybe not. The crown prince would be expected to produce an heir sometime in the future.

But there was no time for reminiscing. And she didn't want to make anyone suspicious.

Tirith's assistant had gone down a list of today's appearances while Maggie had been in the chair of doom, getting her makeup done.

First up, breakfast with Mother. Oh, sure. Run the gauntlet before the first cup of coffee.

Then again, if she could fool Mother, she could fool anybody.

As identical twins, Maggie and Tirith had

switched places occasionally as children. But never for this long. And never when the stakes were this high.

For Tirith. It would be Maggie's mantra as she counted down the hours until she could return to Texas, where she belonged.

It had been more than a decade, but she still remembered the twisting path to the blue parlor, where Mother preferred to eat family meals.

Family.

They hadn't been a family since that terrible day.

Maggie breezed into the room. There was no room for emotion in a breakfast with Mother. Not if she wanted to pull this off.

Mother was already seated at the square table near the window that overlooked a spit of sand that jutted out into the ocean.

There was a time when Maggie had been content to sit near that window for hours, watching the waves beat against the shore.

"Good morning, Mother," she murmured.

Alessandra reached out her hand, and Maggie squeezed it.

There were no bear hugs here, not like the kind Tirith would get from Dad two thousand miles away from here.

"You look tired, dear."

Maggie had to stifle a hysterical giggle as she sat on the opposite side of the table. Had it really only been yesterday morning that she'd sat across from Scarlett, arguing over whether she was too nice?

This breakfast was as different from that one as a Brahma bull was from a pasture of Holstein milk cows.

Fine white linen covered the table and fell halfway to the floor. Exquisite china and real silver tableware were a reminder that she had to be careful. Always be careful.

The staff hovered about, moving silently and efficiently. A young man in the dove-gray palace uniform put a plate of sliced fruit and baked ham and an egg over-easy on the table in front of Maggie.

A young woman poured tea into Mother's cup first, then Maggie's. Tea? Not coffee?

She might only be here for fourteen days, but she might die without her daily coffee fix.

Remembering Mother's comment, she made her lips form a serene smile. Tirith was always serene, wasn't she? "I'm fine."

Mother's eyes were on the spoon she was slowly stirring her tea with. "Your father called."

Maggie's stomach lurched as it had when she was fifteen and had climbed on the back of a steer to feel what it was like to ride a bull. Serenity was hard to fake. "Oh?"

She hadn't thought Gideon and Alessandra still spoke. Everything between them was amicable and mostly handled through Mother's personal assistant.

But the divide was there, an impassable rift wider than the ocean between them. Maggie's fault.

She swallowed hard, but Mother didn't look up to see the emotion she couldn't quite hide.

"He wanted to know if he should come."

Mother's quiet words froze Maggie with that dang teacup at her lips.

But she didn't have time to freeze.

Her teacup rattled in its saucer as she set it down. She folded her hands in her lap, mind racing. Her first instinct had been a sharp *no!* but that would be a Maggie response, not a Tirith one.

She forced out a silent exhale. Tried for a smile, and, since they were talking about Tirith and what had happened two days ago, it was okay that her smile trembled.

"I hope you told him to stay in Texas."

Sorry, Daddy.

Mother's gaze flicked up and then back down. She set her spoon on the edge of the saucer. "That's what I told him."

Maggie was glad Mother wasn't looking at her too closely. She'd borne the guilt for so long that sometimes it lost its sharpness.

Until moments like just now, when she realized how much she'd cost her family. Once upon a time, Alessandra and Gideon had been passionately in love. And once upon another time, Gideon had chosen

Texas, and Maggie, over staying in Glorvaird with his wife and two other daughters.

Although they remained married on paper, they hadn't seen each other in years.

Maggie didn't think she could stomach breakfast after all.

She was about to excuse herself when the door opened and a brunette peeked her head inside.

And then Maggie's baby sister Beatrix was ducking through the doorway.

"Good morning, Mother. Good morning, Tirith."

Bea. If Maggie had been free to do so, she'd have jumped up and embraced her sister. Bea was two years younger. They spoke on the phone weekly, sometimes more, and Bea had come to Texas for a visit during the summer.

Maggie missed her baby sister like a mama cow separated from its calf.

But Tirith saw Beatrix often. Jumping out of her chair like Maggie wanted to would be out of character.

So Maggie sat, even though she ached for that hug.

Her younger sister went to Mother first and got the same hand squeeze Maggie-as-Tirith had.

Maggie waited for the same treatment, but Bea leaned over and hugged her shoulders.

It brought hot moisture to Maggie's eyes, which she quickly blinked away.

"How are you holding up?" Bea asked.

That hysterical giggle bubbled up again, and again Maggie choked it down. "I'm..." She shrugged and then winced internally. Tirith probably didn't shrug.

Bea swiped a triangle of toast off her plate. "Do you want me to go to the ribbon cutting with you this morning? Or maybe you can get out of it...?"

"Not necessary," Maggie murmured coolly. "It won't take long, and I've got my army in place."

Tirith had promised that her personal assistant Elizabeth wouldn't question the request for a second bodyguard in addition to the one that usually followed Tirith around when she was out and about in the kingdom. Maggie wasn't sure she could function with just one. Another sign of Tirith's courage and Maggie's cowardice.

Maggie pushed back her chair from the table. "I should be going."

If she stayed much longer under Mother's watchful eyes, the game would be up.

But Bea followed her out into the corridor, linking their arms as Elizabeth fell in step two paces behind.

Mild panic coursed through Maggie. Did her sister know?

Before either woman could speak, a tall figure strode from a side hallway and toward them like some kind of heat-seeking missile.

"There you are. I'm glad I caught you."
Valentin!

Her cousin, the crown prince, swept both sisters into a hug that rivaled Dad's. And Maggie felt the hot prick of tears again.

Seriously? What was wrong with her?

Being back after all this time was making her off-kilter and over-emotional.

Or maybe it was that she'd always imagined Tirith an ice princess, shut off from real affection and warmth in the family castle.

But that didn't seem to be true. Bea had hugged her. And now Valentin, who walked beside them as they made their way toward the lower level of the castle and the garage, Maggie's destination.

"Annika is attending the naval base celebration with me," he said.

Annika. Annika. Maggie had to rack her brain before she remembered Annika was his current girl-friend. They must be serious if she was attending a royal event at his side.

Or maybe they'd been serious for a while and Maggie hadn't known it.

Tirith was also supposed to attend the recognition ceremony for a general who'd served in the Glorvaird service for three decades.

"She's a little nervous," Valentin said, "so I thought maybe you'd ride in the limo with us and... talk to her." He gave a shrug that Maggie had seen before when

Miles was talking about Scarlett. The one that meant *women stuff*, as if he were baffled.

Bea still had her arm tucked through Maggie's and gave her side an unobtrusive nudge. Was that meant to be a *tee-hee* or a warning?

Maggie had to fight off that hysterical giggle again. Tirith would likely be great at dispensing advice about handling royal events. She participated often enough.

Maggie was hanging on to the distraction her cousin and sister presented. Every time she thought about this stupid ribbon cutting, she wanted to throw up. What was she going to tell Valetin's girlfriend that would ease her nerves?

"I'm sure that's fine," she murmured when it was clear Valentin was waiting for an answer.

He kissed her cheek and went on his way.

When she and Bea reached the garage door, a security guard in a suit and wired at the ear spoke softly into the air and held it open.

Bea let go.

Maggie froze.

Everything so far this morning, all the pretending, could be erased if she turned around now and confessed.

Once she stepped through that door, she was committed to this crazy charade.

Tirith needed her.

And Maggie hadn't come through once before. She'd let everyone down when it counted most.

She had to do this.

She stepped through the door alone.

Luc Moreno was a born politician. His mother had said so when he was a three-year-old standing front of a counter at the sweet shop. He'd cajoled her until she gave in and let him get a treat.

He knew how to get things done. A whisper in the right ear could pave the way when money and intent weren't enough.

And he also knew how to keep secrets.

He'd been a junior councilman for two years. And then after the bruhaha with Father he'd taken a hiatus from serving the public and spent the past two years working tirelessly with his brother Ernest's foundation. Trying to right what Father had done. If things went perfectly, all his work was about to come to fruition. All he needed was one princess to cooperate for another week. Seven days, and the deal would be done.

He stood just inside the sparkling atrium with its glass walls. Waiting for her arrival along with several other people. He'd greeted the hospital director, Nancy, and schmoozed with a parliament member and a photographer who happened to be an old friend from college. A couple other members of the press had been hand-selected and would accompany them inside. More press were gathered on the sidewalk outside, visible through the sparkling glass.

He'd been supposed to meet with Tirith for coffee before this ribbon cutting. She'd texted him early this morning to cancel, and she hadn't said why. His several follow-up texts had been ignored.

And then the royal limo arrived, pulling up to the sidewalk outside. Relief. If she pulled out of the polo match or the gala, he would be doomed.

As usual, the small knot of reporters swarmed the limo door even as the princess's bodyguard shouldered through them to make room for her to exit the car.

And there was Tirith.

Except it wasn't her.

The doppleganger looked like Tirith, but Tirith would never allow herself to be manhandled between the two hulking bodyguards. She'd own the space, even if she were sandwiched between them.

There was something off about her gait. Not a limp, but she didn't walk exactly like Tirith.

And she wore flats. He'd never seen Tirith in flats. Not once.

Which meant this was... Princess Margaret?

He'd never met the reclusive princess who resided in America. Not once in the two years he and Tirith had made plans to be seen together at public events.

Where was Tirith? After she'd ignored his texts this morning, he'd been concerned. Now that he saw this imposter, he was worried. He glanced at the limo but it was already pulling away from the curb.

What was the reclusive princess doing here?

The press shoved microphones in her direction, shouting questions.

"Princess Tirith! Princess—"

The clamor of voices was cut off by the swoosh of the hospital doors closing. The reporters knew better than to follow her inside without an invitation.

The bodyguards faded away, and the Administrator Nancy moved forward to shake the princess's hand. "Princess Tirith, thank you for joining us."

Luc waited for her to correct the woman, but the princess shook her hand with a smile that looked nothing like Tirith's.

How did no one else notice? The truth was as plan as the warm tan on her face, the crinkles of her eyes.

Maybe they only saw what they'd expected to see.

A loud noise from down the hall—a cart spilling over? A metal bedpan hitting the tile floor?—and the princess went from smiling to complete panic.

Her face went chalk-white, and her posture changed as she went from a forced calm into fight-or-flight mode.

Based on the way her gaze was darting about, seeking an escape, he guessed flight was going to win.

He didn't know why she was posing as her sister. Didn't know anything other than he couldn't let anyone get wind that this wasn't Tirith. His brother's foundation depended on it.

So he did think only thing he could think of. He stepped forward, close enough to slide his arm around her waist.

He murmured, "Hello, darling."

And he kissed her.

He felt the infinitesimal stiffening of her spine, and then she was all softness in his arms. She smelled like lavender and sunshine and tasted faintly like strawberries.

He pulled back quickly, aware of the camera snap behind them. He angled his body to shield her from prying eyes as much as possible. He told himself he was protecting her because if she lost her composure, her charade would be spoiled.

But he found himself gazing down into her ethereal blue eyes and realized he wanted to keep holding her.

Which is why he let his hands fall away from her waist.

He couldn't afford to be distracted, not when he was this close to achieving his goal.

There was a noticeable hush in the small group of doctors and administrators who surrounded them as they made their way down a quiet hallway and out to the hospital's central courtyard, where the new cardiac wing would be dedicated. Another horde of people and cameras would be waiting there.

He probably should've thought through that kiss better. *Probably?*

Because kissing her was going to make headlines for sure. He and Tirith were friends, nothing more. Friends who attended events together when having a plus-one was better than being besieged by posers and losers. They had always been careful to be circumspect in public, rarely holding hands. They'd let the public and the press speculate as wildly as they wanted, but they but knew there'd never be more than friendship between them. Luc had been happy with the arrangement, as had Tirith. He'd never kissed Tirith, never wanted to. He'd never felt more than the tiniest twinge of attraction toward the royal princess.

But kissing Margaret?

He'd had his share of first kisses.

And none of them compared to the thrill of that first brush of his hand against her waist.

Kissing her had been electric, pure emotion rising up inside him with no outlet, it was... everything.

What had he just done?

· · ·

Maggie was breathless. And it was no longer thanks to the fear that had gripped her by the throat at the sudden clatter back in the lobby.

She tried the deep breathing techniques she'd learned as part of her recovery, but she could feel the heat of *him* right behind her, and every inhale brought the scent of his spicy cologne.

She'd just kissed her sister's boyfriend. And she'd felt... something.

Maybe she was confused. Her stomach was rumbling its complaints from her skipping breakfast. Maybe hunger had made her knees weak.

That was it. Had to be, right?

She could barely glance at him. But if she acted shy now, he'd figure it out. If he'd kissed her *hello* like that, in front of cameras, no less, he and Tirith must have been closer than Maggie had thought. She'd never asked Tirith outright, just made assumptions from the news articles and web videos the castle staff forwarded to her each week.

She should've quizzed Tirith a little better last night before she'd left Texas. Not that she'd had much time before the royal jet had been scheduled to depart.

Obviously, she needed to call her twin, but now wasn't the time. She was getting ready to step in front of that crowd of people with a giant pair of scissors and smile for the cameras. Shake hands. Be royal.

That was hard enough without worrying about a rogue boyfriend.

She, Luc, and her entourage waited off to the side as a technician fiddled with a cordless microphone and then finally handed it to the hospital administrator.

And then Luc leaned in and spoke so that only she could hear. "Shall we go to lunch after this? Before the board meeting?"

Chapter Two

Luc did not, in fact, have the opportunity to spirit Tirith's doppelgänger away for lunch.

Her personal assistant insisted that Tirith had a previous engagement, which meant that Luc still didn't have the answers he needed. If Tirith pulled out of the gala, everyone who'd paid a premium donation toward his brother's foundation would demand a refund. It would be a complete disaster.

Luc saw the imposter again for the second time as she entered the luxurious boardroom that afternoon. He'd been waiting on her and was the second person to approach after Mrs. Teague, the chairperson.

He didn't miss the microsecond flare of panic in the widening of her eyes as he leaned in close.

But he only brushed a friendly kiss to her cheek the way he would've done for Tirith herself.

He did let his hand linger on her waist.

"Did you have a chance to eat?" he asked. *Where's your sister?*

She began to shrug but halted the movement, and her eyes flicked around the room. "Elizabeth had a salad sent over."

There was something behind what should've been a simple statement. Was she used to heartier food? Coming from a ranch, did she eat steak every day? Hamburgers?

"Your highness."

She glanced to where a gentleman Luc's father's age was approaching them.

She hesitated. It was slight but unmistakable.

"Mr. Hemry." Luc intercepted the man with an outstretched hand.

Hemry gave only a cursory shake, but it was long enough for Luc to note the quick look of appreciation Tirith's sister shot him.

Hemry wanted to update her on the status of the dog rescue they'd spoken about weeks ago. She was all smiles as she listened. Mr. Hemry had no clue that this wasn't Tirith.

He still didn't know why Margaret and Tirith had traded places, but it seemed the princesses wanted to keep it a secret. That he could do, at least until he discovered what was going on.

It was the work of a few minutes for Luc to guide

her around the room, using the names of people Tirith had known for two years in natural conversation. He should've gotten an award for it. He wasn't even sure *she* noticed.

And then Mrs. Teague called the meeting to order, and he slipped into the seat next to Princess Margaret. They'd rounded the long, oval table and ended up on the curve, which meant his knee bumped hers beneath the smooth wooden surface.

The board meeting always kicked off with a discussion of old and new business. Luc's proposal was a line-item on the agenda and would be discussed later.

A delay which gave him too much time to wonder.

His curiosity had been piqued. He always did his research, and the twin princesses were no exception. He'd scoured both the internet and the Glorvaird public library archives before he'd officially met Tirith.

Everyone knew Tirith and Margaret were twins.

But no one knew what had happened when the girls had been twelve.

The two periods of their lives might have been drawn on a white board and bisected with a thick black line. Before twelve and after twelve.

Before twelve, the twins had both lived in the castle. They'd been in the news regularly, along with their younger sister Beatrix. Alessandra and Gideon had lived happily—or so it seemed—at the castle. When photographed, the twins were all smiles, often had their arms around each other, and appeared confident and carefree.

After the girls had turned twelve, Margaret disappeared from the media reports entirely. There was only a small clipping—a paragraph, literally—that mentioned Gideon relocating back to Texas with Margaret. There were no photos of Margaret after that. It was as if she'd disappeared.

And yet, here she was. Sitting next to Luc, so close that his knee was pressed to hers.

There was no mention whatsoever of what had happened when the girls were twelve, but it was obvious something had changed for the royal family.

There should've been rampant speculation in the media, but that was absent too. Had the royal family quashed it? Why? Why was all the secrecy necessary?

And the more important question: was Margaret's return going to interfere with his carefully-laid plans?

On the table before each chair was a blank notepad and pen. A few of the board members had laptops open in front of them.

No one paid Luc any mind as he slid the half-size notepad onto his thigh and wrote on it.

He slipped it on to Margaret's lap, and she jumped. She was nothing like Tirith, who was so cool he'd often wanted to check her pulse.

He couldn't even imagine kissing Tirith. They'd been friends for too long, probably. And when he imagined finding the future Mrs. Moreno—eventually —he had no interest in an ice queen. He'd had enough deep freeze from his father before the man's death two years ago.

So why hadn't he been able to stop thinking about Margaret? Even now, watching her slender fingers pick up her pen from the table made him wonder if those fingers would feel cool against the back of his neck. Or warm, like the woman had felt in his arms.

Margaret was no ice queen.

Maybe like called to like. Maybe he'd recognized her intuitively. He hid his hotter nature—his temper, his passion, the fighting impulses that'd resulted in bloodied knuckles as a teenager—behind the cold politician. But the true nature that he hid had recognized her. Wanted her, even.

Talk about a distraction.

She added something to the notepad and slid it back onto his lap, her attention back on the long-winded Mrs. Devlin from across the table, who was speaking about an art exhibit.

He'd written, *I need to talk to you.*

Beneath his thick-lined scrawl, she'd written in small precise script. *We've just spent an hour together.*

He added another line. *In front of an audience.*

He gently gave the notepad back to her.

She glanced at it, then at him. Her gaze flicked from his eyes to his lips and then down at the paper.

Her lips pursed. Oh ho. *She* was thinking about the kiss they'd shared, too.

Maggie had been doing her level best to think of everything but the kiss.

This man was Tirith's boyfriend, she reminded herself. Even though his knee was pressed against hers, sending fire along every nerve ending.

And yet, she didn't move away.

As the meeting dragged on, she'd forced her mind to wander to her sister instead of to the man beside her.

She needed to remember why she was here.

When Tirith had burst into the kitchen, her gaze had darted between Scarlett and Maggie.

There was no attempt made—by either twin—to hug each other. But Maggie had never seen her sister so rumpled. Her hair was escaping the clip at the back of her neck, and her taupe pantsuit looked as wrinkled as if she'd slept in it.

Maggie came out of her seat. "What's wrong?"

"I—" Tirith glanced at Scarlett. Stopped. Started again. "I need your help."

Scarlett stood from the table and toted her plate to the counter. "I'll leave you to it." She leveled a look at Maggie. "Think about what I said." About using her status to push the charity board around. Not likely.

Tirith had seemed to wilt once Scarlett was out of the room.

"Sit down." Maggie pulled out one of the kitchen chairs, and her sister stumbled into it.

"I've done something. Horrible." Was Tirith... crying?

Maggie lowered herself into the chair next to her as, sure enough, Tirith pressed a napkin to her eyes. She took a gasping inhale. "I was d-driving, and I was d-distracted. T-texting. And I..." She shook her head, pressing the napkin to her face again.

The sisters might not have been close, but Maggie couldn't stand by and see Tirith so upset and do nothing. She put her arm around her sister's shoulders.

She could guess what had happened if Tirith had been texting and driving. A wreck. Or worse.

Why hadn't Tirith had a driver? Her sister rarely drove herself. Or maybe that was Mother. Maggie didn't know enough of their day-to-day life to say for sure.

"I h-hit a pedestrian," Tirith burst out. "A l-little girl."

Oh no. *Oh, Tirith.*

Maggie squeezed her sister. She had no words of comfort. Tirith must have been drowning under the guilt.

Tirith cried into her napkin almost silently as Maggie sat with her.

Finally when Tirith seemed to be calming, Maggie let her arms fall away, resting them on the table in front of her.

"Did Mother send you here?" Maggie asked quietly. If there was a firestorm of media coverage back in Glorvaird, the ranch was as good a hiding place as any.

"I sent myself," Tirith said after a moment's hesitation. "It was very early, and there was no one else about. The palace staff jumped in to handle things and... no one knows, except for the girl's father and the first responders. He agreed to ... to keep things hushed up as long as the family pays for every expense for her."

Maggie's stomach was a knot of tension. "So the girl...?"

"She's alive." Tirith sniffled. She shook her head, pressing the napkin to her face again. "Every time I close my eyes, I see her little face. That moment just before, when I couldn't stop the car..." Her voice squeaked and broke on the last word.

She put down the napkin and grabbed Maggie's wrist on the table, her tear-splotched face fervent in its appeal. "I need you to go back. In my place."

"What?" Maggie's voice rose, the immediate emotional response surprising her more than Tirith had.

But Tirith didn't let go when Maggie tried to pull

away. Her bulldog sister said, "No one knows that I'm here. I can't—can't stand and smile at every ribbon cutting and school visit like there's nothing wrong. I ruined a little girl's life. Forever!"

"So cancel the events." Maggie hadn't been back to Glorvaird since— "I can't."

"Please, Maggie. I've never asked you for anything." Tirith still had that grip on her, but Maggie pulled away and stood, agitation pushing her to pace to the kitchen island and back.

"I made a promise to a friend," Tirith said. "There's a charity ball and polo match, and without my support, his fundraisers will fail. It's really important. I have to be at these events." She cleared her throat. "Or someone that the public thinks is me."

Maggie shuddered just thinking about it. There were reasons—important reasons—she hadn't been back to her homeland in over a decade.

But Tirith was right. She never asked Maggie for anything. Maggie had always been the weaker sister. What did she have that Tirith needed? Nothing.

Except for today. Today Tirith needed a stand-in. A mannequin. A prop.

Tirith played with her fingers, staring at them on the tabletop. "Please, Maggie. My personal assistant will prep you on everything. Mostly you just have to stand there and smile and nod."

Right. Tirith had made it sound so easy. Now,

Maggie shifted in the uncomfortable boardroom seat. *Stand there and smile and nod.* She'd already managed to mess that up in spectacular fashion.

She should never have given in to Tirith's tearful pleas. But she had, and now she was stuck here. *I need to talk to you.* If Luc managed to get her alone, what exactly would she have to do to convince him that she was Tirith?

She hadn't worked out a way to put him off, what to write on the notepad, when he suddenly tensed beside her.

She snapped back to attention. She shouldn't have let her mind wander so far.

Mr. Gower—she thought—had clicked on a slide presentation and was going through the slides in rapid-fire succession. He was rushing so fast that she could barely process the information.

And beside her, Luc's shoulders drew tighter and tighter. Why? Was this a special project of his?

"Excuse me." Maggie was as surprised as Mr. Gower that she'd spoken out of turn. No help for it now. Everyone at the table was looking at her. Her face burned. "Could you please slow down a bit?"

Mr. Gower frowned. "We've seen this presentation before," he groused. But he did slow down as he went through the remaining slides.

The foundation asking for funds provided

programs and scholarships for children with Down syndrome.

"As I mentioned, we've considered this charity before," Mr. Gower said as the last slide clicked off. "It is beyond the scope of our bylaws. We only make gifts to organizations that have been a going concern for three years or more. This foundation"—he tapped a finger on a sheaf of papers on the table in front of him —"has only been viable for eighteen months."

That didn't seem like a good enough reason to deny them. Not to Maggie. What would Tirith do? She didn't even know whether Tirith had commented on the proposal the first time it had been presented.

She cleared her throat delicately. "I'm sorry. I can't remember at the moment. Surely the board has made exceptions before."

Beside her, Luc shifted. His knee pressed against her thigh.

Mr. Hemry joined the conversation. "We have made an occasional exception in the past," he admitted, "but some of our members have expressed concerns about this foundation because of its connection to one of our board members." His eyes swept to Luc and then away. "It has always been important to this board to avoid the appearance of favoritism."

She glanced at the man beside her. His jaw was locked so tight, she wondered if he'd ever pry it open.

"I move to dismiss this proposal without funding," Mr. Gower said.

"But—" She cut off her words at the hot press of Luc's hand on her knee beneath the table.

She glanced at him, but his gaze was far off, somewhere across the room. He squeezed her leg once and then let go.

"We can review the proposal again in a few months," said a woman across the table. Maggie couldn't remember her name. There'd been too many names thrown at her today.

"I move to delay," Mr. Hemry said. It seemed as if he sent an apologetic glance her eway. Was she imagining it?

The motion to delay was seconded, and then a vote was called.

Maggie didn't know whether she should vote or not. She was silent as a chorus of "ayes" echoed around the table. And surprised when Luc joined them.

She ended up abstaining. She could only hope she hadn't messed things up for Tirith after she returned.

And she couldn't help the curiosity coursing through her. She grabbed her pen and wrote on the pad still on her lap.

Why did you vote to delay?

She slipped it to the man beside her.

It was only a moment before he sent it back to her. He'd written only two words.

Politics, darling.

She couldn't help glancing at him. He wore an air of grimness that he hadn't had before.

And she wanted to know why. But if she asked, he'd know she wasn't Tirith.

She had to slip out of this meeting before he cornered her.

Chapter Three

The next day, Maggie checked her phone once more before slipping it into the tiny clutch purse she carried. The phone and a tube of lipstick were about all that fit. Seriously? Who carried something so impractical? Tirith, obviously.

Tirith, who hadn't returned her call yesterday, or the barrage of texts she'd sent this morning.

She'd wanted to talk to her sister before any media photo of that kiss with Luc made it over the ocean to her sister.

Bea had slipped into her suite this morning as the stylists were torturing her in the chair. She'd brought an update on the girl who'd been injured by Tirith's reckless driving.

Since she'd been small, Bea had harbored dreams of being a nurse. She had contacts in the medical profession who'd been able to tell her that the girl was pulling through.

Maggie hadn't had to fake the tears that had sprung to her eyes. She'd been praying for the little girl ever since Tirith had told her what happened. Knowing that the girl would survive was wonderful, though Bea had cautioned there would be a long recovery.

Three hours later, Maggie smoothed the skirt of the flowing pink-patterned dress she'd been tucked into this morning. How long had it been since she'd worn something like this? Maybe a church service, more than a year ago?

A dress like this wouldn't survive ten minutes on the ranch.

She needed to get out of the day limo and walk onto the grounds of the Glorvaird Botanical Society. She'd insisted Elizabeth stay at the castle, afraid she wouldn't be able to hide her terror.

A group of people waited for her, the men in suits and the women in knee-length dresses similar to the one she wore. And hats. She couldn't forget the fancy hats. Hers was on the seat next to her.

It was all too familiar. The trees, their leaves fluttering in the breeze, would close in on her if she stepped out there. The flowers, so pretty from here, would turn menacing. And those pretty dresses and day tuxedos... She hated to think what her mind would conjure with those.

The memories were too stark here. Too close.

She pulled in a deep breath, pushed it out.

Every few moments, someone glanced toward the limo.

Thank goodness they couldn't see through the dark-tinted windows to watch her try to control her panic.

Tirith had insisted this event couldn't be cancelled. Tirith would understand Maggie's fear. If it could have been cancelled, it would have been. Because as important as her sister had insisted it was, Maggie wasn't sure she could go through with it.

Behind the knot of people on the sidewalk, a green lawn was populated with colorfully-dressed patrons. A huge white tent had been erected at the back of the property. And flanking the lawn on both sides would be the carefully-tended gardens.

A garden party.

Nothing to be terrified of.

Unless you were Maggie.

"Just go," she muttered under her breath.

"Your highness?" the driver questioned politely. His gaze flashed to her in the rearview mirror.

He probably thought she was nuts.

He'd be right. She was crazy to have agreed to this.

"Do you want me to go?" he asked.

Yes!

But she answered, "No," on a sigh.

She got out, not waiting for him to come around and open her door. The midmorning heat hit her in the face like a torch. She forced her wobbly legs to carry her onto the sidewalk.

Thank goodness she'd opted for flats again.

Immediately, the knot of people surrounded her.

"Your highness."

"This way—"

She tried to keep her focus on the people, but her vision blurred at the edges. She started to sweat.

"Could I have a glass of water?" she asked no one in particular, but a man peeled off from the group, presumably to find it for her.

She was going to faint. She was going to embarrass herself. Tirith. The entire royal family.

She gasped, reaching out—

And Luc was there beside her, his arm sweeping around her waist.

"Thank you all for your attentiveness to the princess, but if you don't mind, I have to borrow her to say a private hello."

He left the innuendo right out there and received several chuckles even as he swept her away.

She would've been outraged if she'd had any energy for it. As it was, she couldn't catch her breath.

Each inhale was a shallow burst of air that did nothing to fill her lungs.

He held her closely to his side, carrying most of her weight across the lawn. To where?

"Stay with me," he murmured into the hair just above her ear.

What else was she to do? She'd lost motor power over her entire body. Black spots danced in her vision.

And then they followed a flagstone path several paces into a secluded hedgerow. A lovely old tree with a gnarled trunk overhead provided a canopy of shade.

And Luc settled her onto a stone bench that was cold beneath her legs.

"Put your head down," he demanded. And it wasn't as if she could fight him as he nudged her shoulder down with his hand.

"Breathe in. Out. With me." He knelt beside her, inhaled and exhaled slowly until she was matching his rhythm, until the darkness in her vision had receded.

She started to sit up.

"Easy." He kept a hand beneath her elbow.

How was she going to explain her panic attack? She couldn't go back out onto the lawn. Couldn't face all of this. How could Tirith have asked this of her?

Tears pricked her eyes. Her breath rattled in her chest as she fought them off.

"I need a horse," she said on a soft laugh.

And then realized exactly what she'd done. She'd admitted she wasn't Tirith.

Maggie loved horses. Tirith tolerated them.

"I don't think there are any on the guest list."

She stared at him, stunned.

"I've been compared with an unflattering animal numerous times, so I'm probably the best you're going to get." He said it so gravely that it took her a moment—and the quirk of his lips—to realize he was joking.

"You aren't surprised."

He shook his head. "I made you out yesterday at the ribbon cutting."

"Before or after the kiss?" She hadn't meant to ask that, not really.

Something sparked in his eyes, but he looked away. "Perhaps I'll tell you another time." He brought a pointed stare back to her. "Would you like to tell me why I'm hiding in the hedgerow with Princess Margaret?"

"It's Maggie. And I...can't." The story was Tirith's to tell.

"Then perhaps you'll tell me why you suffered a panic attack just now?"

Maybe Luc shouldn't push so hard. She'd barely recovered her breath.

He'd reacted without thinking when he'd been

walking to meet her and saw the panic clear as day on her face. But it was the tears after she'd calmed her breathing that had cracked something inside of him.

Unfortunately, there were five hundred people waiting on the lawn and among the rosebushes, each one eager to shake the princess's hand.

Each one with a pocketful of money to donate to the right cause.

He needed her to go back out there.

He glanced past the guards who'd faded back but stood under the shade tree several yards away.

"I don't suppose Tirith explained what was riding on the next few days?"

She shook her head.

"And she's not coming back?"

"Not for ten days."

He was doomed. Ernest would never forgive him.

But his mother had taught him to muddle through, so that's what he would do. "Can you tell me what happened?"

Her eyes were vulnerable, if slightly distrustful. "My sister knows you. But we've only just met."

He considered her. "True. You aren't certain if you can trust me. But I didn't betray your secret yesterday."

He'd even gone so far as to kiss her to keep it. Yes, that had been a real hardship.

Her eyes narrowed slightly. "And you have some reason for that, I assume."

He wanted to grin, but he didn't. She might've been out of the game, but she hadn't forgotten it. He could work with that.

"Fine. Here's something you can trust: leverage. I know your secret, and I can use it as leverage over you. But if I reciprocate, you'd have leverage, too."

It was a strategic move on his part. Maybe too risky, but he'd bet on her honesty. She wore her emotions too much on her sleeve.

Her blue gaze fixed on his face. Even that was different from Tirith's. Tirith only ever half-listened to him. Her intelligent mind was always a step ahead, always puzzling answers. He'd learned she didn't mean to offend. It's just how she was.

But he almost felt the intensity of Maggie's gaze like a touch.

"Tirith knows my story." Though not all of it. "After my father died, our family discovered he'd gambled everything away, including money he'd stolen from my brother. Money that Ernest had earmarked to start the foundation."

It still hurt saying it aloud. Now Maggie was one of a handful of people who knew. He'd spent the past four years smoothing over the family's reputation and trying to rebuild what his father had destroyed for Ernest and Katie and Guinevere. He'd catered to people he couldn't stand. Curried favors from too many.

And he'd gotten things back on track. Almost.

He needed a princess to walk out on the lawn with him.

He looked at her expectantly.

She exhaled softly. "I want to help you." When she raised her soft, sad eyes to him, he believed her.

"But...?"

"But." She looked away again. "When I was twelve, Tirith and I were kidnapped out of a garden party much like this one."

Everything around him seemed to grind to a halt.

Whatever he'd imagined, it wasn't this. None of the media speculation had even come close.

She must've read the shock on his face, because she laughed softly, sadly. "It was kept from the press."

"And that's why you've stayed in America."

She bit her lip, nodding slightly. "I came back for Tirith. She said she'd made a promise. She just didn't tell me it was to you." Something, some emotion flitted quickly over her expression and then was gone.

And he knew they were running out of time before someone came looking for her.

"Do you think you can face the crowd?"

She kept her eyes down. "I don't know." Those long lashes lifted and revealed the vulnerability beneath. "Would you stay with me?"

"I think I can suffer the hardship."

. . .

One of the first hurdles Maggie had overcome in therapy had been asking for help. She'd learned not to be ashamed to lean on her father, her biggest supporter during those dark days.

She'd grown up. Or so she'd thought.

There was something about asking Luc for help that made her feel sick to her stomach.

She'd promised she wouldn't let Tirith down. Neither would she let him down.

Her mouth felt as dry as a Texas summer day as she stood up from the bench on shaky legs.

She walked beside him, past the hedgerow, and out from the secluded shade into the morning sunlight.

"How's your kung fu?" she asked. Maybe if she kept talking, she'd be able to keep from throwing up.

"Never learned," he admitted cheerfully.

"Ju jitsu?" she asked. "I've taken a few classes but didn't stick with it. No?"

He shook his head.

"What about karate?"

"Sorry." His grin was quick and contagious. "You'll have to rely on your palace muscle men."

There'd been bodyguards that fateful morning, and it hadn't changed the outcome. Darkness and memories threatened to send her back into hiding.

"I can shriek like a little girl. I have it on good authority that it's terrifying."

His teasing voice intruded on the blackness that had begun to take over her thoughts.

He was here, and she wasn't twelve anymore. She was a resourceful, intelligent woman who could train a horse ten times her weight, who subdued rowdy cowhands with a single look.

She was a princess.

Once out in the sunlight, it was apparent she and Luc had been missed. Hordes of people were waiting for them, wanting a press of her handshake or a selfie with her or to mention to her that they didn't like the royal family's most recently policy on healthcare or tax reform or whatever.

As promised, Luc stayed by her side. When the press of the crowd should've separated them, he stepped close and kept a hand at her waist.

And when there was a slight break in the crowd, he leaned in and spoke into her ear. "Thank you for doing this. I know it must be difficult."

He couldn't know how difficult. Every time someone passed by in the edge of her vision, it brought back a flash of memory. Of *that* memory, of being grabbed and silenced with a hand over her mouth.

"You should know that my niece will be eternally grateful."

His words shook her out of the memory that threatened to suck her under. He seemed to know somehow that she was on a knife's edge, teetering between blind panic and hysterical, uncontrollable laughter. Neither was appropriate.

He kept talking.

"She was born with Down syndrome."

Oh. She hadn't known. "What's her name? Your niece?"

It took him a second to respond. "Guinevere. I'm afraid my sister-in-law was a lover of classic literature."

Maggie couldn't help smiling at that.

"The foundation is Guinevere's baby, really. She's seventeen now. My brother is quite a bit older" he added when he must've read the question on her face. "Ever since she was a toddler, she's always wanted to do what the children around her were doing. Whether that meant playing tag or drawing or, when she was older, taking riding lessons. My brother and sister-in-law could afford it, but they also made sure she realized how privileged she was. And Guinevere..." He huffed a half-laugh. "She can't stand for others to be left out. So the foundation was born to benefit other kids like her."

"She sounds like she has a kind heart." Maggie would love to meet her. "Is she here?"

"The kindest. And no. But she'll be at the polo match on Friday. It's a charity match, and the teams are a mix of Guinevere and her friends, professional players, and a few celebrities."

"It sounds delightful. I can't wait to meet her."

"She's amazing." But he was frowning. "Which is why what my father did was unconscionable." He stretched his frown into a semblance of a smile. "But that's not your concern."

Tirith had made it her concern. And Maggie couldn't help wondering why. How had her sister met Luc? How long had it taken her to fall for his charm? To discover the man's true heart beneath?

Maggie had seen enough to know he was someone she'd like to know more. Someone she could fall for—if he hadn't already been taken by her sister.

They were besieged by another large group of patrons, and Maggie kept shaking hands. Smiling. But her thoughts kept returning to Luc.

When she began to be overwhelmed by all of it, he smiled charmingly and joked that he didn't want her to get sunstroke, and then gently guided her to the most private corner beneath the huge canvas tent.

When she sat, he pressed a cold glass of lemonade into her hand. "Halfway there," he said. "Good job on not fainting."

She smiled a little just before she drank from the cup.

"So this is the big secret, hmm?" he said almost absently as he gazed around the area. He stood with the confident ease of someone accustomed to power. One hand rested in his pocket, the lapel of his jacket open to reveal a flat, toned belly beneath. "The reason you haven't been home in so long."

"Glorvaird isn't home anymore," she admitted softly, tearing her eyes away. He belonged to Tirith. Not her.

"How is it the public never found out?"

"There was no need. The ransom demand was made almost immediately and..." She suddenly had to focus on her breathing. In. Out. In. Out. When she could, she smiled for him. "And then it was over."

Such an understatement to encompass those forty-eight terrifying hours. But now wasn't the time or place to talk about such a sensitive subject. There were people circulating all around, though she and Luc been given a wide berth. What had she been thinking, confiding even this much in him?

She pressed the back of her wrist to her forehead. "I've been trying to get in touch with ... with her."

She'd almost slipped up and said her sister's name. Luc was intelligent. He must know who she was talking about. "I thought I should explain to her that"—she dropped her voice—"the kiss meant nothing."

His eyes narrowed slightly, his gaze resting on her face for a moment that stretched a smidge too long. He clapped a hand to his chest. "I'm terribly wounded. Not sure I'll survive this critique on my romantic skills."

She attempted a smirk, but a reluctant smile pulled

at the corners of her mouth. "I don't want any hint of scandal, or confusion, when she comes back."

There was something calculating behind his gaze, but it was quickly shuttered. "As much as it pains me to admit this, your—*she* and I have—"

"Excuse me. Your highness? The second receiving line is waiting." A staff member who looked suitably embarrassed to have interrupted them stood nearby, shifting his feet anxiously.

No more time for talking. Though Maggie wished he'd waited a few more seconds before interrupting.

She and I have ... what?

Chapter Four

"Oh, you're a beautiful one, aren't you?"

Maggie approached the regal palomino, and the groom holding its bridle gave her room to admire the marvelous beast.

"Well, I feel appropriately put in my place."

Luc's wry statement made her want to nuzzle her face against the horse's snout. To hide.

They'd never finished their conversation two days ago.

And as she hadn't been able to connect with Tirith, she was more unsettled than before about her feelings for the man.

Seeing him at today's polo match brought all the emotions from the garden party right back to the surface. Yesterday, she'd spent a hour on the phone with her therapist. Talking through the flashbacks and crazy emotional roller coaster had helped. Or at least she'd thought it had.

But today, as their eyes met across the horse's shoulders, the shared knowledge of what she'd been through was there in his eyes.

"All right?" he asked in little more than a whisper.

She smiled tightly. "I found a horse," she answered.

She'd come out today determined to show him that she wasn't weak. That maybe she wasn't as cool and collected as Tirith, but neither was she as weak as she'd seemed when she'd had the panic attack. She didn't want to admit to herself why his good opinion mattered so.

Across the lawn, tents had been set up for the spectators, who were now gathering. She supposed she was meant to be over there, smiling and politicking.

She didn't want to.

One of the uniformed polo players approached, and she realized for the first time that Luc was in uniform, the dark green checked shirt molding to the curves of his shoulders.

The other player nodded to her.

Luc made introductions. "Princess Tirith, may I present my friend Jean Marc? Jean Marc, her highness."

She accepted the quick handshake, didn't miss the speculative glance she received from the other man.

"I didn't know your highness had a fondness for

horses," Jean Marc said, "or I'd have twisted Luc's arm for an introduction long before now."

Luc slid his friend a sideways glance. "Did I say friend? I meant associate... more of a passing acquaintance, really."

Jean Marc laughed, but then turned serious. "Luc, I have some bad news. Everett just called me from the ER. He had an unfortunate incident with a cake and a flight of stairs."

Luc's smile faded. "What about Roberts?"

"Out of the country," Jean Marc said. He looked to Maggie, making sure to include her. "He was our substitute."

"So we're short a player," Luc said.

"It appears so."

Maggie glanced to the tent where the younger players had gathered. She could see one of the teens speaking animatedly to a couple that might have been his parents.

"Perhaps we can play with seven," Jean Marc said.

"Or I could join," Maggie said.

Jean Marc's head snapped to her, but she couldn't look away from Luc, whose eyes had gone wide.

"Your highness, I did not know you could ride," Jean Marc said in the polite way that she was sure everyone used to mollify her sister.

"I've had lessons," she demurred. "It's a charity match—meant for fun. Correct?"

"I'll see if I can find an extra uniform." Jean Marc left them alone.

Luc frowned. He took her elbow and leaned in close. "Are you trying to be found out?" He smiled and waved at someone across the lawn, but his voice was low and almost furious when he continued. "Tirith isn't known for her riding."

"Our father is a rancher," she reminded him. "It can't be out of the question for her to ride."

He shook his head. "So you'll pretend to be a barely passable rider. Disaster averted."

His sarcasm was not lost on her. "Won't most of the spectators be focusing on the children? That's the focus of today's event, isn't it?"

He sighed. "Princess, it's impossible for anyone to focus on anything but you." He didn't sound happy about it.

"Is this about protecting your event? Or is it about protecting me? Because I don't need your protection." But how could he know that when she'd blubbered all over him at the garden party? Surely he thought she was a foolish, over-emotional woman.

He started to answer, then snapped his jaws closed when a young woman with a bundle of clothing in hand came and fetched Maggie to change.

In minutes, she had donned the uniform of the team that would play opposite Luc's. Good. Maybe a little distance would benefit them both.

Maggie met the green team, shaking hands all around and exchanging pleasantries. And then turned to her own.

A boy of about thirteen introduced himself as Franco. She wondered how he would reach the ball without falling from his horse. "Are you Luc's girlfriend?" Franco asked.

Maggie's mouth opened and closed. She imagined she resembled a fish in an aquarium.

"It's complicated."

They were the very words she'd been thinking, but Maggie wasn't the one who'd said them.

She glanced behind her to see a young woman approach. "That's what Uncle Luc always says when I ask him about it."

"You must be Guinevere."

The girl was smiling and wearing a uniform that matched Maggie's. Her handshake was quick and firm, and she kept on smiling even as the teams were announced to rousing cheers from the crowd.

The horse Maggie was introduced to was a pretty mare with a coat like lustrous chocolate. She let the horse get her scent, stroked its neck with a gentle hand.

The mare was intelligent, comfortable with all the noise and strangers around her.

When Maggie swung up into the saddle, she was almost herself again.

Be Tirith.

She could do this. She just had to pretend she couldn't ride.

"That's it!"

Luc turned at Maggie's cry, which was almost drowned out by the cheers of the crowd as Guinevere knocked the ball through the goalposts.

Jean Marc rode close as they wheeled their horses to the center of the field. "Moreno. Get your head in the game."

Luc glared at him, but he couldn't deny his friend was right.

It was impossible to concentrate with Princess Maggie riding. She'd almost come unseated twice—he had never imagined she knew trick riding—and had fumbled her mallet at least three times. Each time she made an error, the crowd reacted. It was as if they were on the edge of their seats, unable to look away.

Luc knew how they felt.

And the blue team was winning.

Somehow, without seeming to do anything at all, Maggie was passing the ball to her teammates and setting them up for plays that led to points on the scoreboard. And it wasn't only Paul VanGardner, the professional player on her team, who was benefiting from her sneaky maneuvers. She'd diverted the ball to

Guinevere and Franco more than double the times she'd sent it to VanGardner.

The game was playing out exactly how Luc had wanted it to. And Maggie was making it happen. *And* entertaining the crowd.

Maybe he owed her an apology.

The umpire blew his whistle to signal the end of the third chukkas. They'd take a four-minute break while grooms changed out the horses. Then, they'd play the last period.

Luc guzzled from a bottle of cold water, trying to ignore his buzzing thoughts. It was impossible.

Maggie was like no one he'd ever met.

She'd been through something traumatic and yet had braved the garden party. All for him and to benefit his brother's foundation. And now this, today, for Guinevere.

Who had abandoned her team and was skipping over to Luc. "Guess what?"

He never could guess. Guinevere might easily be thinking about unicorns and rainbows instead of the game they were currently playing.

"Tell me, Peanut."

"Princess Tirith invited me to the castle to see the horses there! Isn't that amazing?"

He raised his gaze to connect with Maggie, who stood several yards away. She wasn't paying attention but laughing at something Franco had said. Her eyes shone with true joy.

He wanted that gaze pointed at him.

"Uncle Luc. Isn't it amazing?"

"Amazing," he repeated.

"So you'll take me there? To the royal stables?"

Behind him, Jean Marc was mounting up on his fresh horse and ordering his teammates to do the same. "Moreno!" he bellowed.

Luc brushed a kiss on Guinevere's cheek. "We'll see, Peanut."

For now, he had a match to finish.

Chapter Five

Maggie had been to the Glorvaird Naval Base once as a small girl. She could still remember being awed by the sailors marching in formation, thinking how ugly the squat, brown brick buildings were, smelling the salt even though the ocean was out of sight.

None of it had changed.

Today there was a crowd gathered on a wide expanse of runway. A portable stage had been set up for the ceremony, and several men in uniforms, their chests decorated with medals, stood in parade rest behind it.

Valentin and Annika were having some kind of fight. Maggie had noticed the tension between them in the limo. It had been impossible to miss. Annika had sat with arms crossed, her body angled away from the crown prince. She'd barely responded to the small talk Maggie had attempted. And Maggie thought it was more than the nerves Valentin had mentioned when he'd invited her to today's event.

Now the three of them stood awkwardly silent as the assembly was called to order. Several photographers flashed cameras from the back of the crowd.

A red sports car came screaming up the tarmac, squealing to a stop behind the royal limo with a screech of tires.

The general who was introducing the ceremony went on as if nothing had happened, but heads in the crowd turned to the commotion.

Max, Valentin's younger brother, who stood tall and sleek in a designer suit, got out of the sports car and strode toward them.

Valentin glared, but Max ignored him, offering a dazzling smile to Annika and then Maggie. He touched Maggie's elbow as he leaned in to brush a brotherly kiss against her cheek.

He did the same to Annika, and Valentin's tension went through the roof. He looked as if he wanted to punch his brother.

And then Valentin was called to the stage. A smattering of applause heralded him, and he had no choice but to make his way up the steps to the platform, leaving Max to stand between the two women.

"Who picked out his tie?" Max said under his breath. "He looks like an old geezer."

Maggie didn't think so. She knew nothing of men's fashion but thought Valentin looked sharp in a dark tie with the charcoal suit.

Annika giggled.

Maggie frowned, but neither Max or Annika was paying attention. Max had shifted closer to her and was leaning in to whisper in Annika's ear.

Maggie forced her eyes to the stage. Valentin was delivering his speech with poise and his natural charisma. But then he glanced over to them.

Annika giggled again at something Max had whispered in her ear.

"Shh." Maggie hushed the other woman. Annika hadn't grown up in the public eye. She didn't know how the press could spin something out of control, like her whispering and giggling with her fiancé's brother. It would turn into a wildfire of coverage if it looked like Valentin was jealous.

At least he'd focused again on the crowd, continuing his speech as if nothing had happened.

Max shot Maggie a look, his eyes sparkling with mischief. "Don't be a stick in the mud like my brother."

Annika sent her a haughty smile. Was she encouraging Max's flirtatious manner? It was difficult to tell.

Maggie sent what she hoped was a quelling look and forced her attention back to Valentin on stage.

He was wrapping up, and she clapped along with the crowd as he pinned a medal on the chest of an older sailor. They shook hands, and Valentin came down the steps as another man in uniform moved behind the microphone and began to speak.

Valentin strode to them, forcing his brother to shift out of the way as he moved to stand at Annika's side.

Valentin kept his focus on the stage, his expression blank. But a muscle ticked in his cheek.

Something was definitely wrong.

Max glanced at Maggie briefly. He wore a smirk, one that was entirely out of place. What was his game? Was he purposely antagonizing his brother?

And Annika. Today was Maggie's first interaction with the woman. Surely she and Valentin were in love. They were engaged! A wedding date had been set for next summer.

But wouldn't a woman in love avoid any hint of impropriety? Especially at such a public event?

It's politics. She heard Luc's whisper from several days ago tickle her memory banks. He'd been talking about the board meeting, the interplay she hadn't understood.

Was this politics, too? A power struggle between the two brothers? What was Max thinking?

On the ranch, things were simple. The family worked together to keep the place running, to take care of the animals, to turn a profit. If Maggie had a problem with someone, she talked to that person and worked it out. There were no hidden agendas, no power plays.

If this was what it was like to be royalty in Glorvaird, she'd gladly leave it behind when she returned home.

Chapter Six

Two days before the gala, Luc found himself in a place he'd never been before. The castle stables.

Maggie had kept her promise. Luc had assumed it was one of those things adults said to placate a child. A promise they'd never keep.

But he was learning he shouldn't assume anything with Maggie. Of course she'd kept her word.

She'd called him last night to coordinate the visit, and they'd ended up talking for over an hour. She was funny and open and curious. And he was in trouble, because he liked her. Too much.

Now, she and Guinevere walked slightly ahead of him, talking easily as Maggie pointed to a dappled gray in one of the stalls. She'd worn jeans and a pale pink button-down shirt, which he was sure she hadn't found in Tirith's closet. The tails of her shirt were untucked, and her hair was down around her shoulders.

He could almost imagine her as she must be on her Texas ranch. Maybe add a cowboy hat and a smudge of dirt across her cheek, and the image would be complete.

She glanced over her shoulder at him, wrinkling her nose when she caught him staring.

She and Guinevere moved to the next stall. His phone dinged, and he fished it out of the pocket of his slacks. An email. From Ernest. He let the women pull away as he quickly scanned it.

Even with revenue from the gala, without the funding from the charity board, his brother's foundation wasn't going to make it through the year. It was clear from the text that Ernest was discouraged.

Bitter disappointment surged. Luc had worked tirelessly on the week's events and squeezed funding from every conceivable charity and grant he could think of.

And it wasn't enough.

Maybe he should give up. Ernest could go back to his job in the public sector, but Luc knew he didn't really want that.

A glance at Guinevere, animated as she talked horses with Maggie, was all it took for Luc to know he couldn't give up. His niece would be devastated.

He just needed to think of a stone he'd left unturned. Someone with deep pockets. They didn't need much to meet the foundation's first-year needs. Fifty thousand dollars. It was a drop in the bucket for some people.

"Uncle Luc!"

Guinevere's call pulled him out of his panic-induced brain fog. This wasn't the time to fix his brother's funding problem.

After he dropped off Guinevere, he'd seclude himself in his office and see what could be done.

He joined the two women outside a stall that held a striking ebony stallion with a white blaze down his face.

"Tirith says her father shipped this horse all the way across the ocean as a gift for Princess Alessandra. Isn't he beautiful?"

"He is." A horse like this one was an exceptional, valuable gift. But the rancher and Princess Alessandra remained estranged.

Now that he knew about the kidnapping, Luc couldn't help but wonder what part it had played in the separation.

"Was it a very important message?" Guinevere asked, nodding toward the phone he still held in his hand.

Ah. Guinevere never missed a thing. "Nothing that won't keep."

Maggie's eyes held a soft question, and he shook his head slightly. He'd tell her later about the funding problems. Or maybe not. She was leaving in a few days, and Ernest's foundation wasn't her responsibility. He and Tirith had cooked up the plan to save it together, and Maggie had been gracious enough by stepping in to handle the events in her sister's place.

"Are you and Tirith going to get married?"

Maggie watched Luc react to the innocent question. He first appeared stunned, then his eyes cut to her and away. If she wasn't mistaken, a faint blush rose high on his cheeks.

"No, Guinny. No." He almost sounded choked up.

"But you kissed. I saw it on the telly."

Now the teen looked at Maggie, who grew uncomfortable under her probing gaze.

"Friends kiss sometimes," she murmured.

"Yes! Tirith and I are just friends," Luc said quickly. Their eyes met and held.

She could almost read what he'd left unsaid. *And this isn't Tirith, anyway.*

Maggie was well aware.

Her sister could attend a garden party without having a panic attack. Tirith was cool and unaffected by the social undercurrents that threatened to drive

Maggie crazy. Why couldn't people just say what they meant?

Tirith... Tirith had captured Luc's attention from the beginning. They'd known each other for years.

Most of the time, Maggie was glad she'd gone to Texas, glad she'd been spared the pressure of growing up in the public eye. Right now, though, she realized what she'd missed—the opportunity to meet this man years sooner.

Stupid.

Even if Luc had known them both for years, he'd have chosen Tirith. Calm, relaxed Tirith. Not scared-of-her-shadow Maggie.

She turned her attention back to the conversation in time to hear Guinevere say, "That didn't look like a friend kiss. I played it over three times." She glanced between the two adults. "It looked like a true love kiss."

If Luc had barely blushed before, now Maggie's face was on fire.

And it was only made worse when she caught Luc's intense, thoughtful stare.

"It was an act," he told his niece, almost idly. He didn't look away from Maggie. "For the cameras."

If anything, she blushed even harder. He knew that she wasn't the world's greatest actress. He'd seen it firsthand, though she seemed to have fooled the general public.

She broke the stare and turned to the horse. The stallion Dad had gifted Mother.

The last thing she needed was Luc focused on her feelings for him. Mostly because she still wasn't sure what those feelings were.

She'd fallen into his kiss that very first day.

And she hadn't stopped falling yet.

Watching him with his niece was yet another facet of the complex man. He was gentle with her, and he treated her with respect, never acting as if her questions were silly or didn't matter. Maggie could see how much he loved the girl.

She was afraid she was falling for him.

That would be incredibly stupid. He lived here, in Glorvaird. She was going back to Texas as soon as Tirith returned.

She loved the ranch. It was her home. She hated politics. Hated the power plays that happened every day among the royal family and those who revolved around them. She couldn't stay.

And there was still the not-so-small matter of Luc's relationship with her sister. He'd claimed once that they were only friends, but she'd seen pictures of Luc and Tirith in the media.

What could she believe?

"I'm sorry for my niece's nosy questions," Luc said.

Guinevere had wandered from the stables out onto the grassy embankment nearby. On the opposite side of the castle, huge cliffs guarded the private beach. But here, the grass gave way to sand that sloped gently down to the ocean. Guinevere loved the water, though he'd cautioned her not to go out in it.

He and Maggie hung back as Guinevere outpaced them.

"It's okay." Maggie's head tilted to one side, her gaze far off. He thought they'd been having a moment back in the stables. Guinevere had brought up the kiss, and Maggie had blushed so becomingly that he'd wanted to do it again.

And then something had changed. She'd pulled away, put distance between them.

"She's a doll," Maggie said softly. "I'm going to tell Tirith to invite her to the castle again. Maybe to tea. Tirith will adore her."

It was a reminder that Maggie's time in Glorvaird was short.

He swallowed. "Have you thought about staying? As yourself, of course."

She stared out at the horizon. The breeze blew wisps of hair against her cheek. "I've considered it. But not seriously. Texas is my home now."

He nodded. What more could he say? She seemed determined to leave.

She expelled a noisy sigh and then turned to him.

Her arms were wrapped around her middle, her hands clasping both elbows. "How did you and Tirith meet? I've been curious."

"I tried to blackmail her."

A surprised burst of laughter escaped her. "What?"

Guinevere interrupted, waving and shouting to them from the beach.

"Don't get wet!" he shouted. He kept several large towels in his trunk, though, just for Guinevere's adventures. If she went in the water, it wouldn't be the end of the world.

When it was clear her attention was captured by something at the water's edge, he allowed his attention to return to Maggie, who watched him expectantly.

"Well?" she demanded. "I must have the story now."

He shrugged. "It isn't as dastardly as it sounds. I badly needed an introduction to your cousin Max. For reasons—well, never mind that now. I finagled an invitation to a party I'd heard she would be attending and had a grand plan to approach her. Unfortunately, there was a man hassling her. She'd shaken her bodyguard, and this guy was asking her out, saying how their mothers would think it was a perfect match." He shook his head. "He was... I don't remember. A count or something. It was clear she wasn't interested and that he was trying to push her into it."

She was gazing at him so guilelessly, listening so intently. Maybe that's why he said what he said next.

"I would love to tell you I was the gallant knight riding to rescue her, but the truth is I was looking for a way to get a favor." He wasn't a white knight, even though when Maggie looked at him like she was now, he wanted to be.

"We struck a deal that she'd introduce me to Max if I accompanied her to a school visit. Purely as friends."

Tirith was as mercenary as he was. It was why he'd abandoned his initial blackmail plan—that and the fact that the woman didn't have a single bone hidden in her closet, much less a whole skeleton full—and why they'd become true friends instead of just using each other. When he'd finally confessed to his real mission and what his father had done, she'd supported him. She'd been the one to come up with the fundraising ideas.

"She's got an incredible mind," he said. "She can enter a room full of people and see the relationships, the connections to be made as if the people were pieces on a chess board." And often, she played Queen, moving pieces around the board at will.

Maggie was intuitive and kind and open, so unlike her sister.

He'd asked whether she would stay, but he couldn't imagine her playing at politics the way Tirith did.

Maybe it was why he liked her so much. He opened his mouth to tell her so, but Guinevere had begun her trek back to them and interrupted.

Maybe it was for the best. Maggie was leaving, and if he was very lucky, he'd be working on Ernest's funding for the next year.

Chapter Seven

"Wow."

Maggie swiveled at the voice and came face-to-face with her twin for the second time in less than two weeks.

Tirith closed the door to her suite behind her. "You look incredible."

Maggie had spent a quarter hour staring at herself in the mirror. She didn't recognize the woman looking back at her. The elegant up-do they'd tamed her hair into, the darker makeup.

Mostly the dress. Floor-length, off-the-shoulder, and a pale ice blue. She looked like a princess.

She felt like a fraud.

Where was the cowgirl who lived in jeans and worn-out boots?

What was real? The cowgirl she'd left behind or the princess looking back at her?

Or, could she be both?

She didn't want to leave her life in Texas behind. She loved the horses. Loved her father.

But she hadn't known how it would feel to come home to Glorvaird. So many delightful childhood memories had returned along with her. Things she hadn't thought about in years.

Being in the public eye hadn't been as difficult as she'd feared.

And then there was Luc.

Luc, who'd charmed her and listened to her and *kissed* her.

Her whirling thoughts hadn't resolved when Tirith entered the apartment.

She wasn't sure she hid her surprise. "I thought you weren't coming in until tomorrow."

There were still shadows in Tirith's eyes, though she looked more at peace than when Maggie had left her in Texas. "I need to find a way to make reparations for what happened. The girl's father..." She pinched her lips together. "And... I wanted to be here for the gala tonight. I promised, after all."

For Luc. It couldn't be clearer, though Tirith didn't come out and say it.

Tirith was back. and that meant Maggie didn't need to attend the gala at all.

She sat on the tufted velvet sofa, her stomach roiling. She'd thought she would have one more night with Luc. But now... Now Tirith would be by his side.

A knock at the door revealed Tirith's personal assistant, who delivered two pieces of luggage and glanced between the sisters. She was trained well enough to keep her silence as she left the room.

Tirith removed something small and red from her purse and smoothed it out on the small table beneath the wall-mounted mirror. A bandana.

"How's Dad?" Maggie asked. "Did he discover the switch?"

"In the first five minutes," Tirith admitted with a little laugh. "I convinced him not to tell."

"He called Mother."

Tirith looked up sharply at this information. "Does she know?"

Maggie shook her head. Shrugged. "I don't know. She was very close-mouthed about the conversation. Only told me he'd phoned." Maggie had hoped for more time with her mother, but their schedules hadn't been able to align.

Tirith looked down at the table, smoothed her finger over the bandana. "I didn't think they talked."

Neither did Maggie, though the little girl's hope inside her had never died.

And a tiny voice inside her wondered. If she stayed in Glorvaird, would Dad come back?

Or would he remain in America? Was the damage she'd done to her parents' marriage permanent?

"It wasn't your fault," Tirith said.

"What?"

"Their separation."

Maggie had been away from her sister for so long, she'd forgotten how uncanny the twin connection could be.

"Of course it was my fault. Dad moved to the ranch for me."

Tirith leveled a look on her. "He didn't have to stay. He could've tried harder."

Maggie's chin went up. "Mother could have reached out. Gotten on a plane." She'd witnessed her father's hurt on their first missed wedding anniversary. He'd tried to hide it, but her sensitive thirteen-year-old heart had seen it anyway.

Tirith frowned. "It's too late now."

"It's never too late for love," Maggie murmured.

Tirith's sharp gaze rested on her again.

Maggie turned her attention away from Tirith and focused on the few personal things she'd brought from home. She plucked at the gown. "I suppose I should take this off." She was surprised Tirith's team of stylists hadn't already swarmed the room again. Maybe Tirith had asked them for a few minutes for the sisterly reunion.

Maggie stood.

Her stomach hurt.

"Or..."

She looked over her shoulder to Tirith, who was sending her a contemplative look.

"What if we both attend the gala tonight?"

Could they? But Maggie quickly dismissed the idea. "No one is supposed to know I'm in Glorvaird. The palace would need to make an official statement..."

Tirith shrugged. "It can be made tomorrow. It will cause a stir if we are both announced. Imagine the publicity for Luc and his brother's foundation."

For Luc.

Could Maggie really stand beside her sister? It was the one test she'd hadn't endured yet.

Tirith had been strong for so long, was still being strong, returning for Luc and the foundation when it was clear she was haunted by what had happened.

But if Maggie attended, could she still have her last night with Luc? It wouldn't be the same, not when he'd be at Tirith's side. As it had always been.

But maybe she could find a way to say goodbye.

Luc was standing in the middle of the ballroom talking with a high ranking parliament member when Princess Tirith and Princess Margaret were announced.

Around him, the assembled crowd quieted.

Both princesses descended the grand staircase that would deposit them at the open ballroom doors.

Tirith wore a gown of royal blue. Maggie's was a delicate, floor-length dress of pale blue. Tirith moved with cool, confident elegance. At her side, Maggie took each step with a quiet determination that was etched in the set of her shoulders, the most minute pinch of her lips.

Tirith was beautiful. Maybe the most beautiful woman he'd ever seen.

But Maggie slayed him. She stole his breath and every thought except a visceral *mine*.

A throat cleared beside him, and he came back to himself as the princesses entered the ballroom and the crowd came back to life, instantly swirling around him.

The man he'd been speaking to was looking at him with a sly smile that made Luc remember why he didn't allow his guard down in public.

"Does she know?"

It would be rude to excuse himself, even if all he wanted to do was push through the throng of idiots gathering around the two princesses.

He made himself smile. "Does who know what?"

"Princess Tirith. Does she know you're in love with her?"

He wanted to laugh but was afraid the desperate sound would make him sound crazy. Or give him away.

He wasn't now and never had been in love with Tirith. It would've been so much easier if he had been. They were a decent match, even if his family's coffers weren't what they once had been.

Maggie hadn't a care about politics. Maybe her innocent heart was what he admired so much.

And he knew she'd never settle for him, not when she was happy back in America.

The crowd parted, and there came Tirith, her stride purposeful as she made a beeline toward him. She had Maggie's hand in hers and was practically dragging her twin across the room.

He excused himself from the politician and met Tirith, suddenly feeling strangled by his black bowtie.

"Hello, darling." She greeted him with a kiss on the cheek. As she leaned toward him, her hand gripped his forearm. Hard.

He couldn't decipher the intense look in her eyes. Was she angry? Happy?

Every person nearby was watching them. He and Tirith were supposed to kick off the night with a dance, but Maggie's presence complicated things. He didn't want her standing at the side of the ballroom alone while he waltzed off with Tirith.

Nor was there an easy way to mention this to Tirith, not when every ear around was hanging on their every word.

But maybe Tirith had planned their entrance,

because she spoke loudly enough for those around to hear. "Luc, having my sister join our little event is an honor. Would you escort her around the dance floor?"

"Of course." He'd had to speak past the relief lodged in his throat as he stepped past Tirith and extended his hand toward Maggie.

He couldn't smile at her. His feelings were already too close to the surface.

She wasn't looking directly at him, but she placed her hand in his. Her skin was like warm, like the princess herself.

The string quartet played, and music swirled around them. The crowd faded back to give them room on the ballroom floor.

And he took Maggie into his arms for the first time as herself.

He kept an appropriate amount of space between them when he wanted her closer. *Tirith is here*, he reminded himself. He would keep reminding himself. He didn't want any hint of scandal for his friend. But more importantly, he wanted to protect Maggie.

"Are you all right?" he asked. Alone on the dance floor, for now, no one was near enough to catch his words. It was a shame. If there had been a crowd, he would've had an excuse to lean in closer.

"Of course." A slight smile played about her lips. But it was the lift of her eyes to meet his gaze—the first

time she'd done so since she'd entered the ballroom—
that revealed the turmoil beneath her calm words.

She looked over his shoulder, but not before he'd glimpsed the vulnerability in her eyes.

He wanted to curse. No, what he really wanted to do was fold her into his arms and kiss her desperately, kiss her until every hint of that vulnerability was gone.

He didn't dare.

"Maggie," he murmured. It was the first time her name had crossed his lips.

"Don't," she whispered. She didn't look at him again, not really. Her gaze was on his ear, maybe, or his hair. Everyone watching would see her looking at him, but she wasn't.

Don't. It was the one thing she could've said to wake him up. She didn't want him to make a scene.

She cleared her throat. "Is Guinevere watching from home? Surely this will make the news."

Guinevere. Thank God one of them was keeping their head. It wasn't him.

Maggie liked Guinevere. Of course she wouldn't want to cause drama at an event that could decide the fate of Guinevere's foundation.

Was his niece the only reason she'd joined Tirith for this event? She could've slipped away into the night, no one the wiser.

It was his turn to clear his throat. "You look..." He shook his head as he swung her into a twirl. She came back into his arms. She fit there. Did she know it, too? "I can't find the right words. Everything sounds trite. Tonight, you're the most beautiful woman I've ever seen."

Roses of color bloomed high in her cheeks. "Thank you," she murmured.

"Was it a good reunion with your sister?"

Her glance flicked over his shoulder, presumably to rest on Tirith at the edge of the ballroom. There was so much emotion behind that look.

"I think she'll be okay now." When she returned her attention to him, her smile was a shade too bright. "I left her personal assistant to pack what few things I brought with me. I'll leave in the morning."

He felt as if he'd been punched in the throat. Couldn't breathe. Couldn't speak. And the song was coming to an end.

Ask her to stay. He was going to do it. He opened his mouth to blurt out his feelings, no matter the crowd that was watching them.

She spoke first. "When will you know if tonight's event was enough? Financially, I mean."

The foundation. She'd just told him she was leaving, and she was worried about the foundation. She wasn't thinking about him at all.

Could she send a clearer message? Maybe it was better that he hadn't spilled his feelings for her.

"It won't be." He'd seen the final attendance

numbers already. Unless someone slipped him a large donation check before the night was over—unlikely—come tomorrow he would be scrambling for funds. "I'll figure something out," he said. "It's what I do."

The music ended, and he drew to a stop, letting his hands fall away from her.

Now. Ask her to stay. Beg. But he did none of those things.

He gave her a slight bow. "Thank you for the dance. And for... everything."

He walked away.

Maggie should've left after the dance. No. She shouldn't have listened to Tirith in the first place. She shouldn't have come down at all.

Now, two hours later, she was torturing herself.

She'd tried to let herself be distracted by the myriad of people who'd introduced themselves to her.

But nothing could distract her attention from Luc and Tirith.

Her sister had been poised and collected. She'd directed numerous cheques into Luc's hands, where they disappeared quickly into an inside pocket of his jacket. She did it so effortlessly, laughing and talking with the powerful men in the room, laying a hand on their arm or drawing their wives into the conversation.

Maggie would need years of lessons to learn to work a room like that. Tirith did it naturally.

And Luc was right by her side. Flagging down a waiter to refill her champagne glass when it was empty. Touching the small of her back. Even the way he angled his body toward Tirith bothered the heck out of Maggie.

She was jealous, plain and simple.

And stupid. So stupid.

He'd told her that he and Tirith were only friends. And she'd believed him. Stupid.

How could he pay such attention to Tirith, be so close to her, and not be in love with her?

Maggie had excused herself politely from the last herd of gawkers and now stood at the edge of the ballroom. She really should leave. Go back to Tirith's suite and get her bag. She could catch a few hours of sleep anywhere. Her sister's sofa was as good a place as any.

"I guess you're not staying."

She turned at the voice behind her. There was her younger sister in a simple black sheath with her hair down around her shoulders. Had she crashed the party? She hadn't been announced as an official guest.

"Bea."

Her sister reached out, and Maggie fell into the hug. Tears pricked her eyes. She dearly missed her sister.

"You could stay longer, you know. Ten days isn't

nearly enough."

Maggie backed out of the hug and was blinking furiously, trying to stem her pesky tears, when Bea's words registered.

"You knew?"

Bea laughed. "You're kidding, right? You don't think I could tell you weren't miss prim and proper in the first ten seconds? It's the way you stand," she said all in a rush. "I think it must be all the riding you've done. There's something in your posture—but no one else would see it. Not unless they'd been to the ranch and knew you."

No one else but Luc.

Maggie pushed him from her thoughts. "Did Mother figure it out, then?"

Maggie had planned to speak to Mother first thing in the morning, confess to everything. Drag Tirith with her, if necessary. Smooth things over. But if Mother had figured it out, like Bea...

Bea shook her head. "She's been flustered and out of sorts ever since Dad's phone call. I don't think she noticed."

Shoot. That meant there would be waterworks and a full-fledged guilt trip to look forward to in the morning.

Maggie would welcome the distraction.

She shouldn't, but she couldn't help glancing back to where she'd seen Tirith and Luc the last time.

Tirith was gone, but Luc remained surrounded by a small knot of people. He couldn't have felt her watching, but he look up. Right at her.

Their gazes clashed and held.

And then he looked away, his mouth moving. He was in the conversation.

She'd been stupid enough to hope he'd... what? Denounce Guinevere's foundation and claim he couldn't live without her?

He wouldn't be the man she loved if he'd done that. His niece mattered to him. Helping young people mattered to him.

She'd wanted to matter, too.

As she watched, Tirith returned to the circle. Luc held out a welcoming hand to her, clasped it in his.

Maggie had to look away. Her eyes pricked with tears anew. She had to get out of there.

"I'm a little disappointed," Bea said, startling her. She'd almost forgotten her sister was there.

"Why?" If her voice was breathless with tears, hopefully Bea would be kind enough not to comment.

"The Maggie I know, the one who wrangles half-ton bulls and keeps cowboys in line, would've already walked over there and claimed him."

She looked at her sister, channeling the very best poker face she could manage. "And whom am I supposed to claim?"

Bea's nose wrinkled. "Really? That's all you've got?

You're in love with him."

She'd barely admitted it to herself, but Bea had guessed.

"He's with Tirith," she murmured, looking away. It was too hard to bear Bea's scrutiny.

"No, he's not. They'd always been friends. Nothing more."

She wanted to believe her sister. But her eyes told her something entirely different.

"It's all a show," Bea said. "For everyone here. For the money."

The foundation.

She knew the foundation was important. It's why she'd come to Glorvaird.

But that didn't mean she'd ever fit here. Maybe if she'd never left the castle, maybe if she'd grown up in the bosom of politics and power, things could have been different.

But she wasn't Tirith. She wasn't a princess anymore. She was a cowgirl who valued honesty and hard work.

She couldn't reconcile the two.

That's why she didn't belong here.

She didn't want this life.

"I'm going up to my... to Tirith's rooms. I'll say good-night." She hugged Bea. There would be a tearful goodbye in the morning. For now, she needed to be alone.

Chapter Eight

Maggie didn't find the solace she'd hoped for back in Texas.

Oh, things were the same as a day, then two, then a week passed.

Her father had given her one of his bear hugs, and his worried gaze had followed her for the first few days after her return. And then it had been back to business as usual.

They'd fixed a fence line where years of runoff had eroded the ground. She and Scarlett had argued over whether to sell off part of the winter herd. She'd spent hours on horseback, half the time lost in daydreams of Luc and what could've been.

She was happy. She told herself so.

She just didn't feel it.

And now she was getting ready to walk into the

boardroom for the Triple H Foundation and be thrust into the world of politics all over again.

Only this time, she had a little Luc sitting on her shoulder.

Imagining what he would say and do gave her confidence when Mrs. Evans opened up the floor to old business.

"There's the matter of the equine therapy program," Maggie said.

She was peripherally aware of the boardroom door opening behind her, of someone slipping into a chair against the wall, almost directly behind her.

She didn't look.

She couldn't allow the distraction or she would lose her nerve.

"I think we've devoted enough time to your little idea, Maggie dear," Mrs. Evans said. "And then there was the unexpected expense you brought to us last week.." The woman used the same faintly condescending, *I'm-humoring-you* tone she always used.

But this time it didn't cow Maggie, not with the memory of Luc burning a hole in her gut.

"I appreciate your help in facilitating our meetings," she said. "But I'm still the chair, am I not?"

Luc had taught her the value of silence. She let her expectant gaze drift around the table, making eye contact with each board member in turn.

Two dropped their eyes. She chose to believe it

was in deference to her station. Two gave her faint smiles. And two gave her minute nods.

Mrs. Evans sat with a huff.

Had they been waiting all this time for her to find some gumption?

"My father established this foundation to benefit our local community *and* other special projects."

"Which we did with the gift last week," Mrs. Evans muttered.

Maggie shot her a quelling glance and—miracle of miracles—the woman quieted.

"The equine therapy program is needed," Maggie said. "You don't know my history. I endured something traumatic when I was twelve years old. For a long time, my horse was the only thing that gave me comfort. I couldn't talk to a therapist. I couldn't take comfort from my father. But being with my horse gave me peace. And there are children in our county who need the same. We *will* be moving forward with the program."

No one challenged her. Not in the moments of silence she allowed. Not as she laid out the program and the next steps and demanded buy-in from each board member. Mrs. Evans only gave in grudgingly.

The Maggie from a month ago would've been appalled. She would've accused herself of throwing her weight around.

Scarlett had been right. Maggie had been too kind. So kind, she'd allowed herself to be walked all over.

There was a satisfaction in getting this done.

She should've done it a year ago.

When the meeting adjourned, Mrs. Hawes, who'd been sitting right next to her, turned in her chair.

"I'm glad you decided to do the therapy program, dear." Somehow the way she used the endearment was different from the condescending way Mrs. Evans had. "Your dad will be proud of you."

"Thank you." It was nice to be praised, but she was proud of herself.

Mrs. Hawes tilted her head to the side. "I think your young man is waiting for you."

"I don't have—" Maggie's denial cut off as she turned to look where the other woman had indicated.

Luc.

He was standing just in front of the chair he must've vacated.

Luc had been the one who'd entered the meeting and sat?

The rest of the murmured conversations behind her faded away as walked toward him. She couldn't read his expression. He almost looked... wary?

"What are you doing here?"

What was he doing here? Did he even know?

Taking a risk. A crazy, jump-off-the-skyscraper-with-no-parachute risk.

His heart was pounding so hard that he felt it in his temples.

"Ernest's foundation received a check," he said. "For one hundred thousand dollars."

Her eyes lowered even as her lips twitched.

"From an American charity we'd never heard of before. Imagine my surprise when he told me to look up the website and I saw your picture there."

Her chin came up, and he could see the strength and determination in the set of her jaw. "As you witnessed"—she waved her hand to encompass the room and the board members who remained—"our foundation takes seriously our mission to help others."

He couldn't hold back his smile. He'd witnessed it all right. Maggie had come into her own. He'd been irrationally proud of her as she'd stood up to the board member who'd been running the meeting. Maggie had been magnificent.

He wanted to reach out for her. Wanted to fold her into his arms.

But he wasn't sure he had the right.

"Maggie, can we—?"

"You finished in here, Mags?"

A woman a few years older than Maggie had pushed open the door. She had a toddler on her hip and was noticeably pregnant. Her eyes lit on him, and instant curiosity lit her face. "Who's this?"

Maggie went to the woman, extending her arms to take the toddler.

"Maggie!" The girl patted her face.

Maggie tickled her neck, which elicited a spate of giggles.

Maggie's... friend?... was still looking at him expectantly.

"This is Luc," Maggie said when the silence lengthened.

"I'm Maggie's cousin Scarlett. You came all the way from Glorvaird? Are you coming out to see the ranch?"

He looked at Maggie. "That depends on Maggie."

She was blushing.

"Well, I'll take off and let you two... finish whatever is going on here. I just wanted to find out how the meeting went. Maggie, did you chicken out?"

"She was magnificent." Luc couldn't keep his eyes off her.

Maggie blushed more, if that were possible.

"That's wonderful!" Scarlett said. "I'm so proud of you."

Maggie shrugged off the praise.

"C'mon, booger bear. Let's go." Scarlett reached for the toddler, but Maggie held on.

"I'll carry her out to the truck."

Scarlett scowled. "I'm not an invalid. I can carry my own daughter."

The set of Maggie's chin said she was adamant.

"I'm going that way anyway." She scooped up a leather satchel from her seat and headed out behind Scarlett.

Luc followed the trio out the doors.

He hadn't been able to believe his eyes when he'd driven into town in his rented sedan. He'd expected small, but the town was miniscule. Of course Maggie would've felt safe here. She must've known everyone by name.

And it was hot. It was a good thing he'd packed a bag instead of jumping on a plane willy-nilly, because he'd had to change his shirt. The soaking humidity and heat combined were like nothing he'd ever experienced back home.

Maggie buckled the toddler into a car seat in the back of a huge, four-door truck. It's wheels and under-carriage were caked with mud.

After she said good-bye to her cousin, the woman drove off with a wave.

And then he was just the two of them standing on the sidewalk in front of the squat brick building.

"You came all this way to thank me?" she asked.

"I came because I can't imagine not having you in my life."

Her eyes widened, and she stepped back.

He hadn't planned to lay it out there like that. "Maggie..." He couldn't stand it a second longer. He reached for her, rested his hands at her waist.

She didn't pull away.

"I'm sorry for that last night. At the gala. I should've found a way to extricate myself from Tirith and—"

"I didn't want that." She shook her head to emphasize the words. "I knew how important the gala was for the foundation." Her gaze lowered. "And besides, Tirith is incredible. If you felt something for her—"

"I don't."

When she raised her eyes, he saw the vulnerability in their depths. The questions that he'd put there. "I've never felt more than friendship for her. I never will. My heart belongs to you."

And he'd do whatever it took to prove it, including grovel. "I should've handled things differently. At the very least, I should've asked you to stay."

He raised one hand and touched her cheek. She closed her eyes and leaned toward his palm.

He couldn't resist any longer. He leaned down and kissed her.

It was right, that first touch of lips, without any pretense between them. Her hands rested on his shoulders.

But when he would've pulled her closer, deepened the kiss, she pressed gently on his shoulders and pushed him away.

Her expression was drawn as he looked down at her. Had he read things completely wrong?

"Luc, I have—I care about you. A great deal. But

before things go any further..." She sighed. "Would you come with me? Out to the ranch?"

He'd go with her anywhere. "Of course."

Maggie should have been elated that Luc had come for her. She was elated—and frightened.

She figured the best way she could explain to him was to show him.

He'd joined her in the farm truck, and now they bumped over the cattle guard. She didn't drive him up to the ranch house. Dad would be up there. Instead, she drove down the rutted lane, past the barn. Out to the fields, a quarter mile in, to a hill where a good portion of the spread was laid out in front of them. She got out of the truck, and he joined her in front of the ticking engine.

For a few moments they stood there, look out over the grassland dotted with grazing cattle.

He stood slightly distant from her, his hands in his pockets. "Should I have stayed in Glorvaird?"

"No!" She turned to him, and he faced her, though there was still too much distance between them.

She took a deep breath. "This is what I wanted to show you." She swept her arm out to the side. "My family has a legacy in Glorvaird, but a part of my legacy is here, too. This land. The animals. Even the foundation and the people we help. And my dad is here."

Tirith had said differently, but Maggie knew in her heart that it was her fault her parents had split. If there was any hope of them being reunited, she'd do everything she could to make it happen. And that meant she should probably stay here, with Dad.

"I can't abandon this part of myself."

But she didn't want to live without Luc, either.

Tears threatened, and she closed her eyes against them.

She heard the sound of his shoes in the crisp grass. A moment later, she felt his presence in front of her. He clasped her elbows in his capable hands, brushing a kiss against her closed eyelids. One and then the other.

"Did you hate it so much, then? Being in Glorvaird?"

"No," she whispered, eyes still closed. That's what made this so difficult. "It felt like being home again." Even that last tearful goodbye with Mother had been something she now held close to her heart. "But—"

"Your heart belongs here, too." He brushed his fingers against her cheek, where a tear had escaped. "Your heart can have two homes."

Could it? Was it possible she belonged both here and in Glorvaird?

Luc's voice was slightly amused when he said, "I suppose that when I said 'I can't live without you,' I should've followed that with 'if that means we're in Texas or Glorvaird or Timbuktu, I'll be happy. Because I'll be with you.'"

She opened her eyes, and he was looking at her with such a combination of vulnerability and intensity. "That is"—she heard the catch in his voice—"if you feel the same."

How could he doubt?

"These past few days," she said, "I've barely been able to function. I feel as if half of me is missing."

A slight smile turned the corners of his mouth. "It didn't seem that way at your board meeting."

"Because I was imagining you beside me. You and your politics and your charisma."

His smile was slowly blossoming into something bigger. "You find me irresistible?"

"I find it impossible not to fall in love with you."

His smile disappeared as her words sank in. Her stomach swooped the same way it had when she was tossed from a horse she was breaking.

"I can scarcely believe it," he breathed. "I don't deserve it, I'm sure of that. But I love you so dearly that I don't care whether or not I deserve your love in return."

He loved her.

The knowledge sank in deep, filling all the deep places in her that had been scarred by a decade of fighting her fears and hiding out on the ranch.

He kissed her then, tenderly. Like a man who'd just been given everything he wanted. His gentleness gave way to passion, and she met him there in each caress, each breath.

When they finally had to draw back or risk suffocating, he held her close. She could feel his heart pounding beneath her cheek. It made her smile, burying her face in his shirt. One of his hands was tangled in the hair at the back of her head. The ponytail she'd worn all morning had tumbled down at some point, and her hair was wild around her head.

"When do you have to return to Glorvaird?" she asked softly, not sure she wanted to know the answer. Would they have a week together? A few days?

He chuckled a little, the sound rumbling beneath her cheek. "Ernest fired me."

"What?" She moved back to see his face.

"He said I'd done enough for the foundation, and he could tell I was unhappy and it was time for me to move on. I don't think he expected me to pick up and head for America." Luc shook his head, a bemused smile on his face. "I don't know anything about ranching, but maybe I can help with your foundation. I understand Americans are accustomed to having their pizza delivered by men in truck. Perhaps I could do that. Or... anything, really."

She frowned. "I'll happily let you run my father's foundation," She took a deep breath. "I think it's time for me to think about splitting my time between the ranch and Glorvaird. Being a part of the royal family again, out of hiding. I can do so much good."

Maybe if she returned to Glorvaird, Dad would too. It was a wistful hope...

He drew her close again, his chin brushing her temple. "You'll need a place to rest. Recuperate. And maybe work off some of the frustrations you'll accumulate working with hard-headed politicians. Your Triple H can be that."

Yes. It could work. For the first time, she could see a new future stretching out in front of her. A cowgirl. A royal. With Luc at her side.

Epilogue

Valentin strode down the palace hallway toward his suite. Half his attention was on the sheaf of paper in his hand, a lengthy bill he had only muddled partway through. Every so often, he glanced up to ensure he wasn't going to mow down a member of the castle staff.

The other half of him was buzzing with tension. The same tension that had stolen his concentration in the ten days since he'd blown up at Annika.

He'd felt betrayed by her easy, flirtatious manner with his brother. Embarrassed that others had witnessed the two of them whispering, their heads bent together during his speech on the naval base.

He'd been embarrassed, but he shouldn't have taken it out on her. She'd been distant ever since he'd lost his temper and shouted at her.

He needed to see her, assure her it wasn't going to happen again. It wasn't like him. She could ask his mother, or Dad, or his personal assistant.

He could change out of the monkey suit he wore and go see her. She had an apartment in the city. He could be there in an hour.

He dropped his arm to his side, dangling the bill there as he quickened his pace. Better to fix things with Annika. Then he could devote his full attention to matters of the crown.

The door to his suite was ajar, and his heart leapt as he neared. He thought he heard Annika's voice. Had she come to him? Even better.

But his hands went cold when her voice became clearer, and he stopped just before the cracked door.

That was definitely her voice, murmuring something he couldn't quite make out.

Another voice answered. This one he recognized, too. Max.

Valentin's good intentions flew away like dandelion chaff in a stiff wind. What was Max doing in his rooms, with his fiancée?

Temper rising, he pushed open the door, only to freeze on the threshold.

Annika and Max weren't simply speaking. They were locked in an embrace, tangled together on his sofa. More than an embrace, if their mussed hair and rumpled clothing were any indication.

"What the—?"

Annika broke the kiss and gasped, pushing on Max's shoulders. Her lipstick was smeared, her lips swollen. This was no single kiss they'd shared.

But Max was in no hurry to let her go. Finally, he moved off the couch with the coiled power of a leopard in every movement.

But Max couldn't know he'd enraged a lion.

Betrayal surged, and Valentin wanted to howl. How could his brother do this to him? How could Annika?

"Get out," he snarled.

"Val—"

Valentin slashed a hand through the air, silencing Annika. "Get out. Both of you." He couldn't even look at her. "We're through."

Max wore a self-satisfied expression, and for the first time in his life, a red haze descended over Valentin's vision.

His brother wasn't moving. Wasn't leaving. And Valentin hated him.

He swung, the punch a quick jab that Max couldn't have seen coming.

It floored him.

"You back-stabbiing scumbag. I never want to see you again."

"Max!" Annika cried out and crumpled to the floor beside Valentin's brother.

At the sight, Valentin turned on his heel and stalked out. He didn't know what he'd have done if he'd stayed.

* * *

Thank you for reading THE OTHER PRINCESS. I hope you loved Maggie and Luc's romance. Valentin had his heart broken, but his mother needs him to marry to carry on the royal heritage... What will he do? Find out in THE PRINCE'S MATCHMAKER:

Crown Prince Valentin has no interest in love. He tried once and was burned and betrayed.

But when his mother, the reigning monarch, insists he marry, he agrees to see a professional matchmaker.

His efforts are halfhearted. The best he can hope for is a beneficial match with someone he can tolerate.

Until he spends more time with his beautiful matchmaker. She's kind and funny and down-to-earth. Everything about her draws him in.

But she's a commoner. Not the kind of woman he is expected to marry.

It isn't long before his heart becomes entangled and he must decide if he dares to be with the one woman he shouldn't want...

Also by Lacy Williams

Wagon Train Matches series (historical romance)

A Trail So Lonesome

Trail of Secrets

A Trail Untamed

Wind River Hearts series (historical romance)

Marrying Miss Marshal

Counterfeit Cowboy

Cowboy Pride

The Homesteader's Sweetheart

Courted by a Cowboy

Roping the Wrangler

Return of the Cowboy Doctor

The Wrangler's Inconvenient Wife

A Cowboy for Christmas

Her Convenient Cowboy

Her Cowboy Deputy

Catching the Cowgirl

The Cowboy's Honor

Winning the Schoolmarm

The Wrangler's Ready-Made Family

Christmas Homecoming

Heart of Gold

Sutter's Hollow series (contemporary romance)

His Small-Town Girl

Secondhand Cowboy

The Cowgirl Next Door

Cowboy Fairytales series (contemporary fairytale romance)

Once Upon a Cowboy

Cowboy Charming

The Toad Prince

The Beastly Princess

The Lost Princess

Kissing Kelsey

Courting Carrie

Stealing Sarah

Keeping Kayla

Melting Megan

The Other Princess

The Prince's Matchmaker

The True Princess

His Forever Princess

Hometown Sweethearts series (contemporary romance)

Kissed by a Cowboy

Love Letters from Cowboy

Mistletoe Cowboy

The Bull Rider

The Brother

The Prodigal

Cowgirl for Keeps

Jingle Bell Cowgirl

Heart of a Cowgirl

3 Days with a Cowboy

Prodigal Cowgirl

Soldier Under the Mistletoe

The Nanny's Christmas Wish

The Rancher's Unexpected Gift

Someone Old

Someone New

Someone Borrowed

Someone Blue (newsletter subscribers only)

Ten Dates

Next Door Santa

Always a Bridesmaid

Love Lessons

Not in a Series

Wagon Train Sweetheart (historical romance)